The Night the
Moon Blew Kisses

The Night the
Moon Blew Kisses

Lynn Manuel

Illustrated by Robin Spowart

Houghton Mifflin Company
Boston 1996

For information about this and other Houghton Mifflin
trade and reference books and multimedia products, visit The Bookstore at
Houghton Mifflin on the World Wide Web at http://www.hmco.com/trade/.

The text is set in 18 pt. Bembo
The illustrations are colored pencil, reproduced in full color.

Library of Congress Cataloging-in-Publication Data
Manuel, Lynn.
The night the moon blew kisses / Lynn Manuel :
illustrated by Robin Spowart.
p. cm.
Summary: As a little girl and her grandmother walk
on a snowy moonlit night, the child blows kisses to the moon
which sends frozen kisses to them in return.
ISBN 0-395-73979-9
[1. Grandmothers — Fiction. 2. Moon — Fiction. 3. Snow — Fiction.]
I. Spowart, Robin, ill. II. Title.
PZ7.M3192Ni 1996
[E] — dc20 95-24391 CIP AC

Manufactured in Singapore
TWP 10 9 8 7 6 5 4 3 2 1

To Nana, with love

L.M.

To Kie who loves kisses

R.S.

In the moonlight,
along the water's edge,

Grandma and I
walk together
in our long, woolly red winter scarves.

Grandma stops
to look up
into the night sky.
"The moon looks lonesome,"
she says.

I think my grandma is right,
so I press my fingers to my lips
and gently blow a kiss

up, up, up
into the cold night sky,
up, up, up
into the wind,
up, up, up
to the face of the moon.

A swirly kiss, a twirly kiss,
a willowy-billowy
wisp of a kiss.

I ask my grandma
if the moon will blow a kiss too.
"I fancy so," she says.
"I feel it in my bones."
And I feel it in *my* bones.

Every now and then
the pale moon
peeks down at us
through the trees
and I blow another kiss
from my fingertips.

A laughing kiss
for the tip of the nose.

A gentle kiss
for the cheek.

A good-night kiss
for the brow.

Grandma and I step out
into a clearing
near the icy-cold water.
The night sky is a-flutter
with silvery flakes of snow.

One touches the tip of my nose.
Another, my cheek.
A third, my brow.

Slowly I turn to Grandma
and smile.
My grandma smiles too.

And, oh, how we laugh
as frozen kisses
melt against our faces!

Swirly kisses, twirly kisses,
willowy-billowy
wisps of kisses.

In the moonlight,
along the water's edge,
Grandma and I
walk together
in our long, woolly red winter scarves

while the moon blows kisses.